FOOLS SHOULD NEVER MARRY!

by

Lil Miss

DORRANCE PUBLISHING CO
EST. 1920
PITTSBURGH, PENNSYLVANIA 15238

Dorrance Publishing Co
585 Alpha Drive
Pittsburgh, PA 15238
Visit our website at www.dorrancebookstore.com

ISBN: 979-8-8860-4352-5
eISBN: 979-8-8860-4448-5

Fools Should *Never* Marry!

There are all kinds of fools. The ones mentioned in the Bible. The ones spoken of by men.

Well, in my case, the man I married got his training from a man who did what he wanted, when he wanted, without regard for his wife's feelings. He set very bad examples for his children to follow. He was a fool. So my husband has that mental attitude, using women to get what he wants and do what he pleases, never having an apology. He's a fool.

And me, I'm another kind of fool, a fool in love with a fool. A fool who says and does nothing, just sits by and allows him to do whatever he desires as long as I don't rock his boat, then he won't turn into a raging idiot. He doesn't want anyone, that means me, to ask where he's been.

I ask, "Can you pay this bill?"

His response: "I don't ask you where you go."

It doesn't take a genius to read between the lines.

Keeping to myself, keeping my feelings inside, keeping my distance, no touching. Stay on my side of the bed. The feelings of love and intimacy are dead. So, who's the fool?

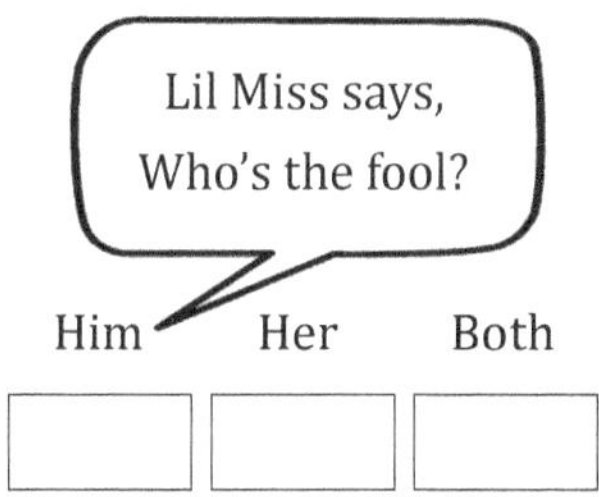

The Things That Hurt the Most

Being in a relationship where there's no communication. A relationship where what you say, you want me to hear, understand, and keep my thoughts to myself, and if I speak you get louder and louder. So, I shut the hell up. My head hurts from the loudness of your demands and commands. So I'm not the one to keep talking. I just shut down, and within myself I'm no longer around. I just shut down.

I pray before I say anything to him, which is hardly ever. The last time, I just wanted you to know how your actions make me feel. As a woman and a wife, I too have the right to voice my opinion.

But what really hurts the most is that we don't have anything in common. So "opposites attract" doesn't always work. I would like to do things together. We don't.

The toll on my soul is hindering me from the joy of being in a happy, healthy marriage with a man whom I had hoped wanted the same thing, but I am sadly mistaken. The walls have been shaken. The city has fallen. The home is in ruins. That's sad, and that's what really hurts: me being a fool, trying to hold on to a disappearing shadow. What a fool, wasting my time, losing out on life, the joy of living. Who's the fool!

How Many Years Are Full of Tears?

How long have I been done wrong? How many days have I been alone? How many nights will you take flight?

Too many to mention. Done wrong by your speech. Many days I've been alone. You leave and don't return; no call, not even answering your phone.

Your response: "I forgot I was married. I'm used to doing what I want when I want."

Many, many nights you've taken flight, you drove like you were in a race for life up, Highway 75, the only one who matters, not wanting to be bothered by me at all. No woman can rule you, can handle you, or can show you any kind of control. So you roll, you rock, you shot out. You praise yourself, you're the man. You show everyone that you rule your world.

But you look like the fool you are because your so-called family and friends respond to your approval in your face, but they talk about you behind your back.

For thirteen years, you pretended to be a real man, knowing how to treat your wife. They are at home. But you are the fool away from your wife trying to be Mr. Big Stuff.

Why?

Being married doesn't make you happy. Marriage can strip away your love, your affection.

You begin to wonder why.

A husband or a wife should communicate. Can't relate, turning your words into a sharp knife, stabbing you, making you year after year feel the pain of despair.

Why? You try to show by your actions, your speech, your kindness, that you really want our love to grow, but your kindness is taken for weakness. Why?

All these years have passed, and you feel so empty, so full of pain, with nothing left to gain, and your tears fall like rain. Why?

I don't know why anymore. I am going to get myself together, keep serving God. He's a happy God, and he wants all his children to be happy. Why did I let another human rob me of my joy? Why has my life been so empty, why didn't I stick to my God so close that no one could take away my joy?

Why?

I see myself as happy before, living a life of peace, with no distractions of a person who's selfish, unthankful, not knowing how to say "I'm sorry." Thinking that their way is okay regardless of your feelings of why.

What happened yesterday is gone. Why? Because I now know that if I don't put God first, I will always fall by the wayside.

Who's the fool?

The Fear

The change all of a sudden. The hostility. The threats. The uneasy feeling that I have my thoughts of being in fear of being alone with you.

The feeling of something taking over your thoughts, your feelings.

The look on your face when you look at me. The feeling from that look sends fear through me.

I'm not a scary person, but you are not the same anymore, and I'm always on guard around you.

You don't care what anyone says when they try to encourage you in the right way.

You don't care what anyone says. Things will be as you want them and that's your attitude with anyone who tries out of love to readjust your attitude.

There is a gloominess about you. There's no spark of joy left in your soul.

You seem so dark in your manner of life. The change is seen very clearly by those who know you and those who don't.

What has happened to you? What could have caused such a sudden change?

If something happens to me, I hope someone reads these pages and investigates my demise.

I pray that you go your way; any day soon will be okay.

Marriages should be "Till death do we part," but not "The way that I feel I could go."

Who's the fool?

My Thoughts Are Unsettled

I keep thinking, *what have I done?*

What actions could I have done differently?

Is it me? If so, why does it always seem to get better when I give in?

I get tired of the fussing, cussing, name-calling, getting put down.

Nothing I do sits right.

So I give in to get some peace of my mind. I apologize even if I'm not wrong.

Then you get all bigheaded like you have won again.

My thoughts are unsettled because even though you are calm, I feel that I had to say I'm sorry for whatever reason, just to get peace of mind.

Just so I can rest, eat, and sleep without your hateful attitude.

It's not easy to be with the fool who thinks they are always right. Not caring how anyone feels as long as things are going their way.

Hating to come home, when I'm the main person trying to keep things together. No thanks, no appreciation for what you have.

It's as if someone owes you something.

You are the man, the one who should be showing me that you care enough to be kind, loving, and understanding. Being a person with a positive attitude for others, trying to learn the right way to keep peace.

Who's the fool?

Humans Are Created to Love

We as humans were created with the need to love and be loved. It is easy to become discouraged if this need is not satisfied for any reason.

How can two people who marry not love one another?

What other reason should you marry? And if you don't love the person, why marry?

If you have the mentality that you are always right, why pretend otherwise before marriage and then change after marriage?

Where's the love? Deceit is totally unacceptable. That's not love. You are truly a fool.

Now that you have done and said all the right things to fool the person, they fall in love with you, hook and line.

Then your true colors come to the fore after marriage. Not long after, you got what you want.

So you won the game, but the war has just begun.

Who's the fool?

I'm Myself

Not trying to please you, not trying to hold in my emotions, I'm myself.

I feel free. I can smile from the heart. I can sing, dance, just feel wonderful.

I feel as I did before we joined together in marriage.

The sun is brighter. The rain feels so good on my face.

My heart is free of distress, pain, and the feeling of being squeezed very tightly.

Wow! I can't believe the way I feel; it's like I'm young, footloose, and fancy free.

I can't believe how great I feel.

I'm actually overjoyed. I feel like dancing, jumping up and down.

Man. This is a wonderful day, okay. I want again to play, turn into a potter's clay.

The mold is broken.

Free at last, free at last.

I can't believe that I allowed myself to let another human being get my feelings so focused on his peace of mind, his happiness at the cost of losing mine.

Who was the fool?

I Feel Special

Once again, I feel special. I put on my fancy nightgowns, my sweet perfume. I feel like a very special person.

When you were around, you never noticed me when I dressed in my very cute, fancy nighties. If I walked in front of you, you would look the other way. You never said anything to make me feel like I was special.

But it's okay. I feel special, and I will wear my fancy gowns from now on. I don't need you to make me feel special. You took that feeling away by your actions.

But I don't need you to make me feel special. I am special. I'm beautiful. No one can take that away but the person themself, by letting others make them feel unhappy about themselves. Being in that type of relationship can be detrimental to some in longtime relationships. But some come to their senses and get back to themselves. I'm back, and a very proud, special lady.

Who's the fool?

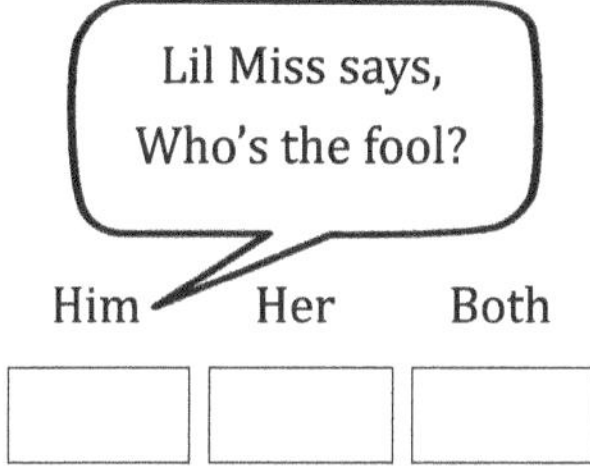

Why Must I Feel Bad?

The pain I feel when you stay away. I feel bad when you went into the room when I woke up. You have been in the back room since last month.

I feel bad when you leave the living room without a word, going to your room.

I feel as if you are just a roommate.

I can figure out why I feel bad.

I never asked you to leave the room we shared together as a married couple.

We were never close; we were never warm and close in any given situation, but at least I knew you were there.

I guess I feel bad because even though you always needed your space, you don't like to be touched. You only like to talk, always a one-way conversation; no one else's conversation interested you unless you were getting something out of it.

I feel bad because I don't know how to say anything that won't set you off.

So I just go day by day, praying, talking to God. He always listens; he never wants to overpower me with loud speech to drown me out, to make me be quiet.

I feel bad because keeping silent to keep the peace is the hardest thing I've done.

Not being able to express myself.

I feel bad and alone, hurt and rejected.

Who's the fool?

Can't Hold Back the Tears

Just sitting here watching a movie alone at home. Out of the blue, I feel tears running down my face.

I pray to stop. The pain I feel I don't understand. What have I done to hurt so deeply?

I start to do a puzzle, find-the-word type.

I'm almost finished. There are thirty-two words to find. I'm just a few words short of finishing. The tears are flowing once again. I pray again to stop. In a few minutes, I stop.

So now I pick up a Bible study book. I get the Bible and look up the cited scriptures. Around paragraph six, I start crying once again.

I pray again; the pain in my heart deepens; the tears flow faster.

I persist in prayer. My soul feels release, a calmness comes over me.

I've worn myself out. I'm tired. So I shower, get dressed for bed.

Thanking God for the comfort I've received.

My tears have stopped. The pain in my heart is gone.

My tears have been held back.

The power of prayer is awesome.

Why Do I Have to Suffer?

Suffer how, you ask? Well, if you must know.

First of all, I don't feel any comfort when I need help. If I'm sick, no response to help is given.

Second, when I keep all the finances up to date, it's never enough. I'm blamed for anything that he doesn't have, or that he wants but doesn't have the money to get.

Through all the years of marriage, would you believe only nine (1-2-3-4-5-6-7-8-9) times in one year were we engaged in a marriage relation all? The other years were less.

Fourth. I asked him to just take me once a month to a fast-food place for breakfast, lunch, or dinner. What are three items on the dollar menu? Never happened.

I could go on, but I'm getting upset with my own self. I could kick my own behind.

So why? Not even good enough to be a part-time lover, which I would never do. But this is a poor excuse for a marriage. I've tried everything to make it work.

So why do I keep putting up with this type of treatment?

Who's the fool?

Questions That Seem to Have No Right Answers

Why do we try to hold on to a relationship that one partner is trying to disrupt?

Is a marriage that's so hard to keep on track by one person worth the time?

What causes a good person to take the foolishness of a fool?

Is it worth the pain and suffering to save a marriage that's doomed?

How can one person save a marriage?

How can the one trying to do all the right things show the other their errors?

When will the one that's suffering realize that their hard work was in vain?

What kind of fool will try and give their all for a lost cause?

Tell me why, when, how can a fool like me get a grip on true happiness and let go of pain and suffering?

Suffering that's been going on for years, shedding so many tears, in this marriage?

Who's the fool?

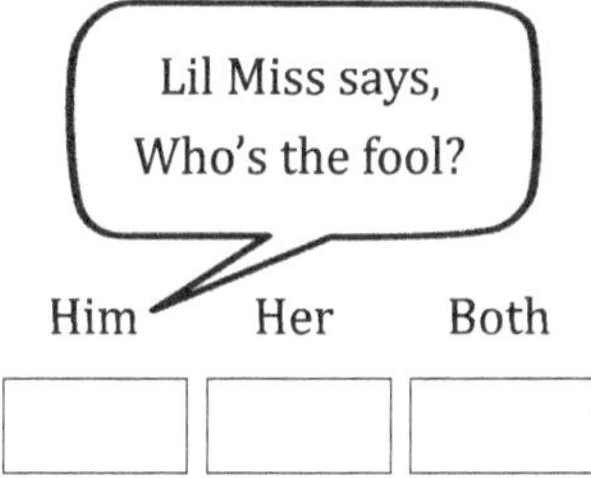

Him   Her   Both

Read Between the Lines

Have you ever tried to have a conversation with someone who responds like this?

Example:

"Honey, can you pay the water bill?" (Which is twenty dollars.)

Their response: "Can you pay the auto insurance?" (which is $145.00).

What do you read into that?

Example:

"Honey, where have you been?"

Answer: "I don't ask you where you go."

What do you read into that?

Example:

"I was worried. Why didn't you tell me you were going out of town?"

Answer: "I forgot I was married. I'm used to doing my thing my way." (By the way, not even an "I'm sorry.")

What do you read into that?

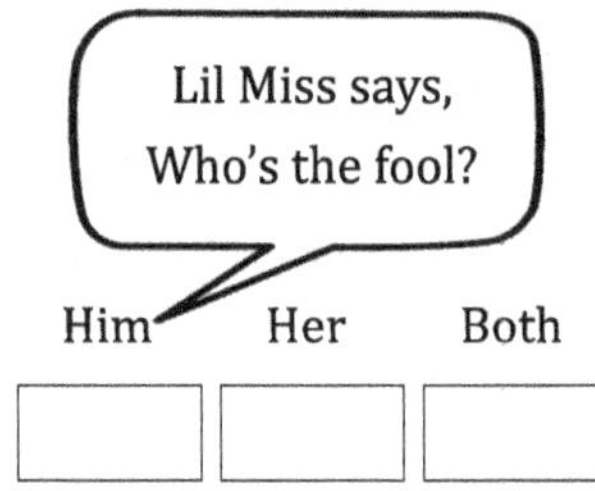

Could Not Win for Losing

I'm not able to hold a conversation that I start, and when it's over you wonder why you even opened your mouth.

Well, this happened to me so many times that now I don't even start to talk about anything. I let the other person, the mister of the house, start and finish all conversations.

Keeping peace is important for me, and it works for him because he wants to be in total control.

Then I'm not accused of telling him what to do, not asking him anything he doesn't want to talk about.

I'm not allowed to be too interested in what he does, where he goes, how much money he has, not anything that has to do with him and his business.

So having a nice, calm, sit-down conversation is long past in this marriage.

Nothing that has to do with my eye, my feelings, or my concerns is of any interest to him. They are off-limits. It's a far distance for a decent response on my behalf on any subject.

So I stay in my room, he in his.

But I tell you this. I'm glad I don't have to be distant with God; he's always there, he always listens and gives me answers in a kind and loving way.

Who's the fool?

Mind Games

Do I look like I was born yesterday? You've been throwing change on the bed for years, stating to others that you give me money when you work.

When I sold my house, I bought you a truck. You tell your family in my face that you just bought yourself a new truck, knowing in all these instances that I would not embarrass you in front of your friends and family. Oh! You would. Well, this is what happened. He turned on me, stating, "Oh, so I never buy anything? What about the new shoes and clothes I bought you?" Not telling them that you dumpster-dived, washed the clothes, and cleaned up the shoes. My response was, "Where did you get them?" Your response is, "Those aren't the ones," leaving out that they were in a bag on the ground with the tags still on them, by the garbage can.

Who would they believe? Me or their family member? Now that's why they directly dislike me; he talks bad about me behind my back and in front of my face, so I never go with him when he visits his family.

I'm known as a wife who thinks she's all that by his family.
Who's the fool?

A Man Just to Have a Man

I heard a woman say one day, "A piece of man is better than no man." And at another time, another woman said, "I just need a man, just to say I have one. I don't want to be an old maid, 'cause we all need someone to love."

I don't know about anybody else, but not all males are men or even grow up to be a man.

Never too late to do the right thing. Can't change a person.

First of all, that man or woman can't love anyone, not even themself, if they don't first love God, who teaches us how to love ourselves. And if we truly love God and ourselves, then we can love someone else.

Practice kindness, goodness, and putting the other person first, not thinking too much of oneself.

If that's not in a marriage, it's a very sad situation. That means someone's selfish, only thinking of self in all aspects of life. Their life, no one else.

You say no one tells you what to do. Does that mean God, too, 'cause he says a man should love his wife as himself?

Do you curse yourself? Do you disrespect yourself?

Think about your actions. Would you like it if someone treated you in the same manner? Does that make you a man?

Who's the fool?

Validation

Why must another person validate another?

Validate—to prove to be valid or strong, sound, and well-grounded on principles or evidence.

Check out the word, the meaning.

So how can someone else prove these things about you? Don't you know yourself whether you are grounded solid in your life or not? Your outward appearance can show only what you want it to portray. Who are you on the inside? What are your personal principles?

We as people, man or woman, should know by now how to validate ourselves. If not, why get others wrapped up in your life when you don't even know who the heck you are? Validation is personal. If we don't know who we are, how can we bond with another who's also lost within their selves? What's the point?

Who's who? If you don't know, how can I know!

Know yourself within, your thoughts. Are they like scrambled eggs or are they solid like a rock? Are your actions erratic? Or are they stable, accountable, or sure footed?

Validation is very important in being a well-rounded adult. If not, you are still a child in an adult frame, having tantrums.

Who's the fool?

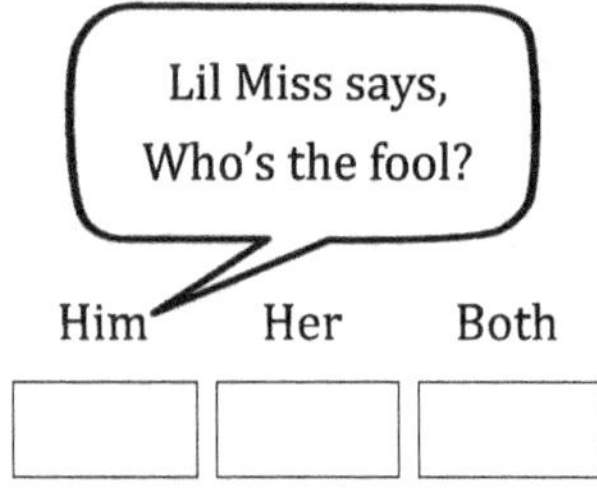

Him   Her   Both

Don't Ignore the Red Flags

Sometimes the answer is right in front of your face. But all we see is that one; oh, it's the one, my soul mate. But wait, their friends and family are telling you things you need to and should know. Oh no, you get all upset and defend the person.

But these people have known him or her all their life. How long have you known them? How long have they been working on your affections?

All you see is the good times. Stop and think, analyze their motives, the action that they took when a certain disagreement came up, or a statement made that went against the grain, so to speak. The look you got when you disagreed with something they said.

Some of us are so quick to jump at the first one who seems to show so much interest in us. But why? Who started it? Where did they come from? How did they get so close so fast?

Are we that desperate for love that we jump at the first one who seems like your soul mate? Why the hurry? What happened to the last one? Just because he or she says it was the other person's fault and they expound on the reasons doesn't mean it's true. Investigate. Small children are smart. They will ask why.

Who's the fool?

We Are Not True Friends

What is a true friend?

Can I count on one of you to listen to my concerns?

Will you listen without a hurtful response?

What is a friend if they aren't even kind enough to let you finish without them taking over the conversation? How could you be a friend if you belittle me every chance you get to anyone who will listen?

And how could I be a true friend to you if I don't make you aware of the wrong course you are taking?

True friends look after each other. They respect each other.

Being married doesn't mean we have to stop being friends.

Being true friends is a way of life, not something to turn off after marriage. That friendship should grow even stronger as the days grow longer.

Who's the fool?

Anger's Like Throwing a Stone in a Hornet's Nest

Leave anger out of the equation. Marriage is hard enough when the two can't agree on much when they don't enjoy spending time together. The first love they had is gone.

No more communication. No more compassion. Just dry air; hard to breathe when you are both in the same room.

No kindness, hurtful comments, rude responses. Loud, uncontrolled outbursts.

That stone, that anger, caused more trouble than was needed.

Anger is an attribute that needs to be kept under control.

Think before you speak. Even pray before you open your mouth. Get a calm spirit, keep your thoughts, speech, and responses in check.

Why upset the hornet's nest?

We should do our best to keep the peace.

Keep the stones of anger outside where they belong.

Who's the fool?

The Polar Bear

My own personal definition of a person who's like a bear: you have to stay downwind so they can't smell you. I'm that person trying to stay downwind from the bear in the house with me. You try to build a wall, some type of protection that keeps out the polar bear, the man. I have built a wall up to keep him out of my space, to protect my feelings, my mind, and my soul.

Some say what they would do differently from me. But I have to maintain my sanity in a way to keep my good standing with God; that's more important to me than any human polar bear in this house who will never go away or find another way to live in peace with himself and others.

Who's the fool?

I Can Do Good by Myself

Many say I can do bad by myself. Well, here's bad: angry words directed at me any time it pleased him.

Not assisting with money issues at all. Cooking, eating, wanting whatever you want when you want it.

Coming and going when and wherever you wish for however long without a word to me.

Not wanting me, your wife, to question you about where you go, when you'll be back, or how much money you have. You get the point. Nobody tells him what to do. That's just a small example of the bad.

Now I can do good by myself. I can rest in peace, sleep the entire night with no interruptions.

I don't have to hear constant complaining about me, what you want, what you don't have, what you need, how tired you are of being married. How you wish you were in Atlanta.

Not walking into a hornet's nest someone else threw a rock in before I got home.

Oh yeah, I'm enjoying my peace; my good times are here. The strain of trying to stay on good terms with a polar bear who thinks his way is the only way is over. Ching, ching.

Who's the fool?

Him Her Both

A Few Last Questions to Myself

If you lived where you could get anything you wanted to eat.

Where you could come and go at will.

Where you did not pay bills.

Where you always had an opinion but did not ever want a response from me that your word was law.

It was your way or no way or even the highway.

What are you tired of? The good life? What part of this marriage caused you to be ready to leave?

I'm the one who should be tired, the one who had to contend with the unhappy dealings of your way or no way.

But it's over, you're gone, find another fool to allow you to do the things you do. I'm through.

Who's the fool?

Lil Miss Says

In these trying times, long-lasting relationships are hard to come by. These days, please take your time. Don't rush into any relationship blindly. Listen to good advice; learn his or her habits. Think with your mind, not your heart.

Sincerely,
Lil Miss